Kofi and the Butterflies

Sandra Horn

illustrated by Lynne Willey

Africa World Press, Inc. P.O. Box 1892 Trenton, NJ 08607

Kofi loved butterflies
more than he loved
any other creature.

He spent hours
watching them
in the park.

He loved the way
they darted and dived
and danced in the air.

He loved to look
at all the different
colors and patterns
on their wings.

Sometimes,
if he was very quiet,
he could get so close,
he could almost touch them.

One day,
as Kofi stood watching the
butterflies,
he caught sight of a boy
catching one.

The butterfly
was struggling to escape
from his net.

It was trapped.

Kofi raced over to him.
'Don't kill that butterfly!'
he shouted.

'That's cruel. Leave it alone!'

'I'm not cruel,
I collect butterflies,
and this one
is for my collection,'
said the boy
in a self-important
sort of way.

'Lots of butterflies
are extinct.
The only way we know
that they existed,
is from collections
like mine,' said the boy.

Kofi thought
for a moment,
looked at the butterfly, and
recognized it.

'That butterfly
is a swallowtail,'
he said quickly.

'I saw one in the museum
on our school trip.
I did a project on them.
They're dying out!
Only a few are left now!'

'Are you sure about the
museum?'
asked the boy.
'Yes I am,'
said Kofi quickly.
'Course I am.'

'Well,' said the boy,
'if you say so.'
He hesitated, lifted the net
and ran off.

The lucky butterfly
stood stock still,
and then fluttered away.
She quickly vanished among
the flowers.

Kofi settled down
to see if more butterflies
would appear.

As he waited,
he heard a small, soft,
squeaky noise.
A beautiful butterfly
which had been
watching the boys,
landed on his shoulder.
'Many thanks, friend,'
squeaked the butterfly.

Kofi was amazed.

'Will you accept
a special invitation
and come with me?'
squeaked the butterfly.
'Be my guest in the fantastic
kingdom of the butterflies.'

Kofi *was* so surprised,
he could only mumble
'Y-y-yes please.'

He began to shrink
immediately.

'Climb on,' whispered
the butterfly,
and off they flew,
higher and higher
into the air.

The wind whistled softly
as they traveled.

After a few minutes,
they came to a huge gate
which seemed to be made
of oak.
It blocked their path
completely.

Kofi thought that they'd
come to the end of their
journey.

But ...

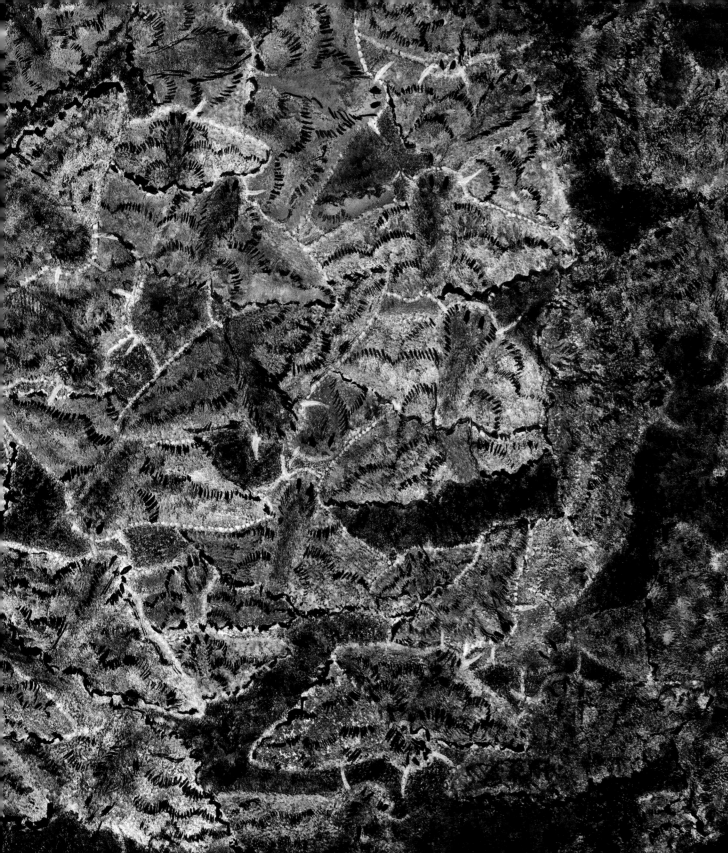

... 'Away!'
cried the butterfly
and the 'gate' became
a fluttering mass.

Kofi caught a glimpse
of a bright,
exciting world beyond.

They flew straight in.

The butterfly landed.

Kofi dismounted
and was suddenly back
to his normal size.

He was in the
most fantastic room
he had ever seen.
At the far end
was what seemed to be
an enormous, stained glass
window.

'Our special guest
is invited into
the inner chamber!'
cried the butterfly.

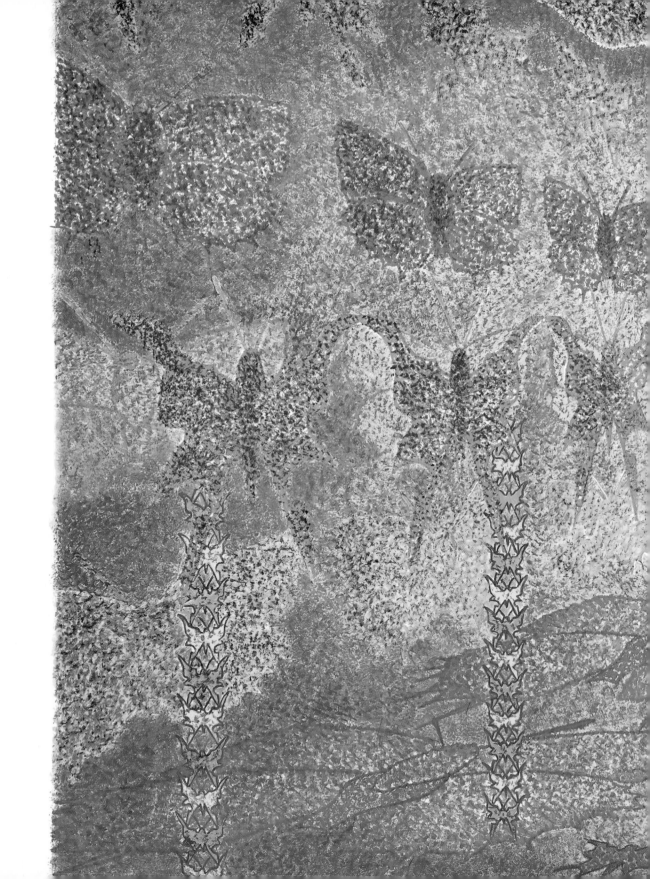

As Kofi watched,
the entire window
seemed to sway
this way and that,
and then fluttered away.

'*AWESOME*'
whispered Kofi.

Then all of a sudden,
a beautiful, blue butterfly
landed on his finger.

'Welcome, kind friend,' she said
softly.
'Your wise words today
will help save us all.'

'Oh, no problem,' muttered Kofi,
wishing he could think of
something fantastic to say.

She then took him on a tour
around the beautiful butterfly
kingdom.

'Thank you,' said Kofi.

'Thank you, Kofi,'
whispered the blue butterfly,
and pressed something
into his hand.

Before he had time
to look at his gift,
he felt himself
shrinking again.

'Climb on!' said the
butterfly once more.

Off they flew,
away from the land
of the butterflies.

As they fluttered
fast through the air,
Kofi whispered, 'I'll
never forget this.'

'Sorry,' said the
butterfly as the wind
rushed by.
'You will not remember
any of this
once you get back.'

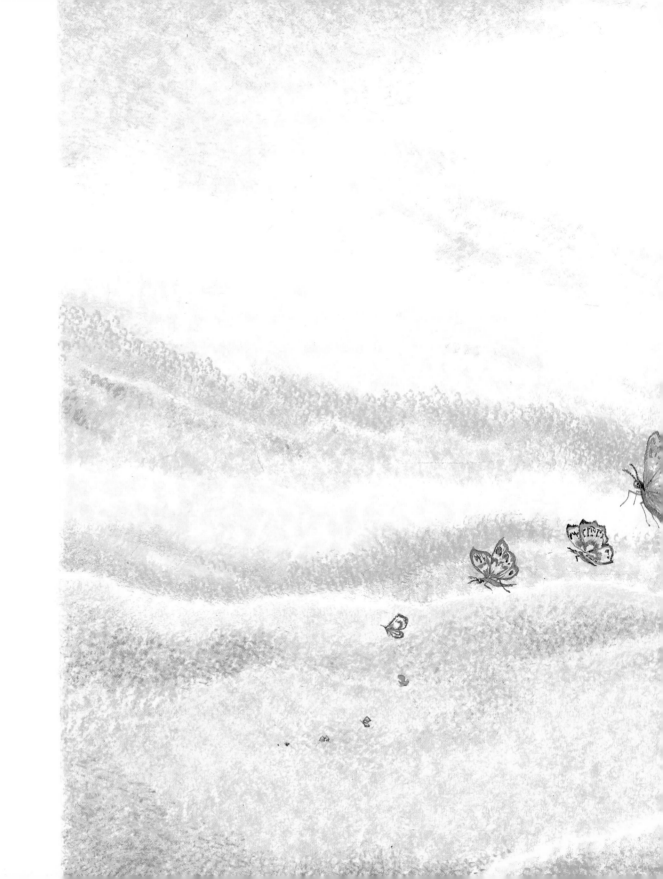

Suddenly, they landed.
Kofi was back
in the park again.

'I must have fallen
asleep,' he thought.
'And that was a really
amazing dream.'

As Kofi rubbed his eyes,
something fell out
of his hand.
He picked up a tiny key,
stamped with a beautiful,
blue butterfly.

'Was that really a
dream?' he thought.

'Well, I wonder ...'

It is estimated that there are over 700 species of butterflies resident in North America, 63 of which are common varieties. In the last thirty to forty years, one half of these have declined in number, and today, twenty-five percent of all species are endangered.

There are many reasons why there are fewer butterflies alive today. We have built new roads, houses and factories on land where butterflies used to live and breed. There is much pollution. Farming has changed the landscape; there is less 'wild' countryside than there was. Also, unfortunately, some people still like to collect butterflies and display them in cabinets. This used to be a common hobby many years ago when butterflies were more abundant. Usually the only butterflies collected nowadays are the very rare ones and this can lead to their total extinction. You should never hurt or kill any butterfly.

We can do a great deal to help protect our remaining butterfly population. We can give advice to people about what is best for butterflies in our gardens, farms and parks. We can protect rare species by buying areas of land where they live and maintaining them as Butterfly Reserves. We can learn more about what butterflies need by studying them.

The best way to help is to join butterfly conservation societies and learn more about these beautiful insects.

Africa World Press, Inc.
P.O. Box 1892
Trenton NJ 08607

Copyright © 1995 Sandra Horn
Copyright © 1995, illustrations by Lynne Willey
Kofi and the Butterflies © Tamarind 1995
First Printing 1995

ISBN: 0-86543-518-9 *Cloth*
0-86543-519-7 *Paper*